To Manu with love
T&JP

First published in 2004 by
Orion Children's Books
A division of the Orion Publishing Group
Orion House
5 Upper St Martin's Lane
London WC2H 9EA

Text © Tony and Jan Payne 2004
Illustrations © Emily Bolam 2004

Designed by Tracey Cunnell

Printed and bound in Italy

ISBN 1 84255 169 8

PLUMMET

Tony and Jan Payne

Illustrated by Emily Bolam

Orion
Children's Books

Plummet had a smile once.

It was a big, happy, stretchy sort of smile . . .

but then he lost it.

Plummet was a Flying Frog. Flying Frogs don't
sit on lily pads all day . . . like some frogs.

Flying Frogs climb to the tops of trees . . .

and

jump

off.

All except Plummet, that is. Plummet had
lost his smile because he couldn't fly.

One day, when he was not looking
where he was hopping, Plummet
bumped into another Flying Frog.

'Sorry,' he said and turned to move away.

'Don't go,' said the little frog, smiling.

'My name is Be-Bop. I'm going to climb up my special Mimosa tree and then fly down. Do you want to come with me?'

'No thanks,' said Plummet miserably. 'I'm going to look at that stone over there.' He pointed to a stone lying at the edge of the lily pond.

Plummet would have liked to play
with Be-Bop, she was nice.

But he was scared to tell her that he couldn't fly.

'You must be really clever!' said Be-Bop.
'I'm playing in trees, while you have
an important stone to look at.'

That made Plummet feel bad. He didn't like telling fibs. Being a Flying Frog who couldn't fly was awful!

Plummet thought of all the times he had tried to fly. He had tried very hard.

He had tried running fast and flapping his arms up and down.

He had tried wearing a Captain Superfrog costume.

He had bought himself an old flying helmet and jacket.

He had made himself wings from birds' feathers.

Nothing worked. Whatever Plummet tried,
he always ended up in a heap on the ground.

But now here was Be-Bop. When she said,
'Grabbit gribbit krack, krack pip!'
Plummet thought he had never heard anything
so nice. She spoke Froglish, of course.

'You have a nice voice,' he said. But he knew she
could never be his friend. He was a Flying Frog who
couldn't fly. Plummet's face went pink with shame.

'I can't fly!' he said in a rush. 'I can't be your friend.'
'Now I know why you look so sad,' said Be-Bop.

'I've never told anyone before,' said Plummet.
'I've tried and tried but all I can do is sort of glide.'
Be-Bop knew something that Plummet did not.

'Come with me, Plummet,' she said.
'I want to show you something.'
Be-Bop took Plummet by the hand
and led him into the forest.

They followed a shady path through tall, dark trees

until suddenly . . .

the trees opened into a beautiful, sunny space filled with thousands of flowers. A magical place.

'Look up,' said Be-Bop softly.
Plummet looked up . . .

'Yee-haaaaa . . .!'

From high in a tree, a frog threw himself
into the air. He spread out his hands and feet
and glided gently to the other side of the clearing.

'That's what I do,' sighed Plummet.
'That's what we all do!' Be-Bop smiled at him.

'You don't fly?' Plummet said.
'We don't fly. It's just a name, Plummet.
Someone must have seen us gliding and
thought we were flying. So they called
us Flying Frogs. Come on. It's great fun!'

Plummet started climbing.
It was easily the best day of his life!

He had a new friend and . . .

something happy and stretchy was
spreading slowly over his face.

Plummet's smile was back!